Elegiac Machinations

Daulton Dickey

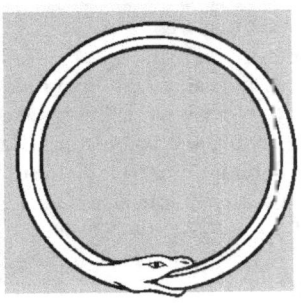

Exeunt REASON Books

This is a work of fiction. All the characters and events portrayed in this novella are either fictitious or are used fictitiously.

This book was—probably, but don't hold us to it—printed on acid-free paper, so licking it will not make you trip. If you purchased the ebook, and you just licked it, then you are—probably, but don't hold us to it—already tripping. If that is the case, then tell us what colors taste like; we're curious.

Also by Daulton Dickey
A Peculiar Arrangement of Atoms: Stories

ISBN: 0692459294
ISBN-13: 978-0692459294

This book is dedicated to my wife, Alice, for putting up with my bullshit.

[1]

The horror of the city on fire, the roar of the city on fire, the smell of the city in flames, and the sight of faces and demons, of multi-pronged-shaped things growing and vanishing inside the flames, fill my head. Dread floats in and out in waves. Everything will eventually collapse and fall to ashes—it's nature's way—and few of us will be surprised by the chrysanthemums wilting on the horizons. Imagine it: empty domes bubbling and imploding, people racing and screaming, marionettes and acrobats swinging on veins hanging from clouds. Wings will sprout from each particle and wave launched by the sun. The particles and waves will slam into the earth, crowning the surface with newspaper print.

People walk in reverse interact in reverse race backward from work across town back home into the shower where water is sucked into the showerhead and back into their beds.

This movie plays eternally.

Flesh glimmers. Sounds shimmer. Colors sing and hum, screech and cry. The textures of waves smacking eyes will paint new layers of soil into which blastocysts are planted—and from them children sprout. The children will grow to absorb programming which will integrate them into the machinery of routine. They'll march through cities, from home to work, spending their free time fighting dreams.

[1.2]

The earth lies supine and grudging beneath the bulk of mechanical earth, fields planted by our species to counter our meaninglessness. Buildings shimmer and glow; they fill cities, islands, oceans. Dust and decay splinter and dissipates in a maze of skyscrapers. The wind authors symphonies, rehearsing and fine-tuning them in gaps between buildings.

The world is an organism into which cells swarm and reproduce. The cells erect forests, lining avenues with artificial oaks, dotting the landscape with steel and chrysanthemums, as they assume to embody 'progress.' But consciousness and delusion are the only differences between cells in a human body and the human cell in the world body. Delusion is a consequence of consciousness, which enables the human cell to peer at itself, to find patterns—sometimes even when patterns aren't present.

[1.3]

A man sits on an apple in a park, gnawing on a plank from a bench. He's wearing hats on his knees and a kneepad on his head. A group of bicyclists pass him—the bicycles: screaming chunks of metal—as they race to collide with the intersection. The man coughs or clears his throat whenever a bicycle passes him.

He drops the plank, clamps a match between his lips, then presses a cigar to the match. Shaking the cigar, he tosses it to the ground and glances around as he mimes pulling smoke from the match.

[1.4]

They see what they want to see. We don't fit their conception of reality, so they choose, and probably not consciously, to overlook us.

How do we break through?

It's like evolution: gradual. But we'll affect them if we keep at it.

Sometimes I believe that.

But sometimes I don't.

I'm here every day. Every day I'm out here doing this. And no one ever looks at me, and by that I mean no one pays attention to me. But they see me, whether they acknowledge me or not. And so I keep doing this. Every day. And then one day I won't be here. Maybe I'll be sick, maybe I'll be married or famous, or maybe I'll be dead. Then the people who walk by here every day, the people who see me without registering me, will notice something's different. They probably won't know something's different, but they'll feel it. The way you do when you leave the house and forget something, but you can't for the life of you remember what you forgot. And so it bugs you. One day, my absence will elicit that response. These people will continue to come by here, to pass through here; and whenever they do, they'll feel this haunting, nagging sensation. And some of them will hopefully start to think. And some of those hopefully will begin to evaluate why they pass through here every single day of their miserable fucking robot lives.

[1.5]

The sun pivots in the linoleum centered tile above the clouds. Ashes heap laughter onto troves of schoolchildren tramping through puddles of coins and one hundred dollar bills. The zen-like face of a maggot blooming in winter steals the gravy from a tub of stool buried inside a cradle. Rocks roll, tumble, as cars float away, distant and bereaved. And the lake of mourning swells in the morning as doves mutate into fish and float to the surface for one last gasp.

Lion heads emerge from nubs on my wrists; they gnaw on metal, ashes, fists. All good poetry twinkles the eye of dead sheep and llama. It floats to me, flows in me; but it's flat and empty, deprived of tone.

The streets bend and bob. Cars float away; they kiss buildings and streetlights. The world trembles in orgiastic ecstasy. I shiver. My head grows dentures, which gnash at particles igniting the air. Beneath me, clouds fuck and merge into a corset of anger. The streets spill into the heavens as cars slip into whirlpools and fade away.

The fields of the sky bare footprints and smears and cataclysmic epiphanies. A woman floats toward me atop a candle dripping into a river of concrete. She smiles. Her teeth drip, forming pools in the nape of her neck. Mouth is opened and disengaged: the black and red of her silence bleeds into the horizon of a Monet.

—See it now? I say. —It's become undone.

—Center the snail.

—But where do we go from here?

—Sky is baking in the nude.

—You see it, then?

Her head implodes: the skull vanishes, her skin floats down and beats against her chest—a soft portrait of ecstasy.

Smiling, she points to something below: a woman lying naked on a rock floating through the sea. A fish emerges from a pomegranate and transforms into a pair of tigers, and they lunge at her.

[2]

The sun is out but hides in a cave of clouds. Raindrops smuggle it to earth. Birds scream. Engines roar as they push, pull, tug cars along, down the road, past sidewalks. Here, there, everywhere—people move and sway. Cattle in calls fall in line. It's the American Dream. Hallucination. A nightmare. People work to spend to work to live in debt. Desirous of the next new thing. Everything is holy if you can obtain it. If you can touch it. Every action is noble if it helps you obtain the latest gadget, the latest orgasm, a kind of intellectual intercourse milking juice from advertisements and pop-psychological propositions.

People move like robots; their actions are mechanical. They move and play with phones or gaze off, devoid of thought. Sky cracks open, clouds part. The sun breaks through, the great and beautiful, the mystical and holy sight of light particles and waves funneling through gaps in the clouds, drenching the crowds, illuminates everyone. People shield their eyes or tilt their phones or lower their heads, furrowing their eyebrows. Everyone ignores the sun's breakthrough, the routing of the clouds; everyone's annoyed by the burst of light; everyone's moving and swaying and marching with downcast eyes, as if the sun is an enemy—or a distraction. But the sun is indifferent. It sun gives you what you need whether you want it or not.

Gum is stuck to the sidewalk. Feet slap it or the concrete beside it.

A bird skips over the gum. It jumps onto a windowsill, leaps to the roof, slips into a hole in the soffit. And no one notices. No one watches the bird, examines its movements. No one stops to applaud or to appreciate the beauty of the ballet of its procession.

Across the street, a man has stopped in the middle of the sidewalk. He's kneeling, looks like he's praying. People pass him without noticing him. They diverge and converge. He stands and falls into line. The line proceeds, and the man is lost in the crosshatch of meat and clothes, of sunglasses and smart phones.

Smoke puffs from the roof of a building not far from where the crowd devoured the man; it catches a ride on the wind, drifts over the crowd and across the street, slamming into—and passing over—me. Smells of scorched meat waft and merge with the crispness of the vanishing storm. The sun wants to come out, tries to break through. It penetrates the clouds, but the clouds fight back. They amputate the light by sealing their wounds.

Then shapes like faces bleed from windows and slip into the light and travel across the street. They bleed and breed in more windows. The street is now a corridor lined with death masks staring out from windows on buildings lining the sidewalk. No one seems to notice them. People walk by, locked in their worlds, lost in impulses firing through their brains, feeding on chemicals and electrical transmissions while neglecting the face-like shapes gazing out at them.

The faces seem almost communicable, like they can latch onto the wind itself and float—shadows growing in fog, transplanted from window to window, xeroxed and carried along and deposited in every reflective surface, even in the sunglasses and eyes of strangers passing without wisdom or acknowledgement or comment.

The air, cold and crisp, fills my chest, freezes the hairs inside my nostrils. The face-like shapes dissolve in my lungs and seep into my pulmonary tissue; they take a joyride through my circulatory system. Faces surf along the breath escaping my lungs. They break apart and dissolve overhead.

[2.1]

Her hair is red and, from a distance, looks brittle, not dirty or greasy or even frayed, but it looks delicate somehow, as if touching it would shatter it. It sways in front of her chest, it curls and lays on her shoulders as she leans forward and slips a spoon into her mouth. She drags the spoon away from her lips. Her eyes, once slit, now spread and blossom—flowers unfurling at the onset of day.

Elbows on the table—who needs etiquette?—she flips through a tattered paperback. She pauses midway between flipping a page and gazes outward, in thought maybe, and settles her eyes on me.

I break my gaze, glance out the window behind her, squint as though I'm studying something.

Face-like shapes linger in windows across the street. But they're fading now. They fade. And when I sense the woman has turned away, I glance at her again: the remnants of a smile drift from her lips. She slurps a gulp of soup. Flips the page. Her eyes bounce from left to right, crawl down, and bounce from left to right again.

The muscles in her shoulders and jaw ripple. She rubs her right shoulder as she reads. Then she arches her spine, cracks her back, and stretches her arms. Below the table, her shirt rises like curtains opening on a stage. Her belly, white, seems firm yet somehow soft, though it's probably my imagination. The cramp or spasm or whatever vanishes. She releases her shoulder, goes back to her book.

She slips the spoon into her mouth again, slurps again, flips the page and massages her shoulder again. The rhythm of her motion, the beauty of her movements, spills into the air, crashing, screaming; and it sings. It sings. No one else seems to notice. The waiters and waitresses, the men and women stuffing their faces, the strangers crisscrossing the sidewalk out front—no one notices or acknowledges the poetry of her motion.

Up out of my chair, I glide across the room and stop at the table, knocking once to snag her attention. She moves fluidly: shifts her gaze from the book to my face while rolling her shoulder blades in a semi-circle. Uninterested and unconcerned, eyes full yet empty— unaware or uninvolved.

—Must be good, I say, gesturing to the book.

—I've read better.

—What is it?

—Lolita.

—Nabakov could churn out prose.

—But the book itself is overrated. Reams of repetition. Someone better could say this in twenty-thousand words.

—But no one else could have said it the way he did, which is why we read good fiction.

—This isn't good.

—Good fiction evokes a response.

—Harlequin novels probably evoke a response.

—Then I'd say it's good fiction, too, I say. —
What you want to, or should, avoid are books that don't
elicit anything. Those are the dangerous ones.

She closes the book and tilts her head.

—If you're hitting on me, she says, —I'll give
you points for technique.

—I'm not hitting on you.

—Then what would you call it?

—An invitation.

—To what?

—A walking tour of the city.

—I'm familiar with the city, thanks.

—Not the city I can show you. I extend my hand,
palm ceilingward. —It's too nice to sit indoors. And I'm
willing to wager that you, too, can show me a new sight
or two. So come on. What do you have to lose?

[2.2]

A lower case 'i' is an Arabic '1' with a dot over it. The eIe
is a lower case 'i' with an eyeball in place of the dot. You
can see the eIe on buildings and street signs, on
overpasses and stoops, on sidewalks and buses across the
city. From north to south, from east to west, the eIe stares
at you, follows you, seems to track every move you make.

I point to one on back of a billboard. It's as tall as
a person. The woman, Alice, considers the vandal,
wonders how he or she had managed to put the eIe up
there.

—That's part of the magic, I say. —You can see
this thing, and you can ask how or why. And either way
you're doing the artist a favor. You're caught in the trap
he, or she, devised.

—But what's the point? I see these things everywhere, and I don't know what they mean. Are they even supposed to mean something?

—It's kind of like subterranean propaganda, the agit prop of the underground.

—I still don't see the point.

—Emblazon the image in your skull. That's the point, I say. —Subconsciously you'll begin to associate this image with something.

Around the corner, and another eIe is the first thing we see. This one is smaller, about the size of a fist, painted below a corporate logo.

—So this is what you wanted to show me, she says. —Graffiti?

—Street art. It's street art.

—It's not new, whatever you want to call it. I see it every day.

—But how often do you acknowledge it? do you think about it?

She looks forward, shakes her head.

[2.3]

We're sitting on a bench on a sidewalk overlooking a rundown building. Cracks and potholes scar the street. The sidewalks are broken, shattered. Weeds grow from the cracks, tower over the uncut grass. Stencils and murals and tags cover the front of the building, an open-air museum free for any- and everyone who sets their eyes on the art, on works of countless men and women. And so people cross the street, ambling down and up the sidewalk, crossing in front of the building, walking alongside the walls, gazing ahead or staring at phones or tablets, or shielding their eyes from the sun. But no one glances at the walls. No one stops to consider or to appreciate the subject or the force of the images splayed and sprayed and preying on the building.

—Look at them, I say, —huddled over there, oblivious.

The people passing the building huddle around a bus stop, an aluminum skeleton with a corrugated roof. A wall bifurcates a bench inside the skeleton. Ads are plastered on the wall. People are sitting on the benches— men and women, young and old. Two teenagers are cackling. One, a boy, points his phone at an advert, what from here looks like a movie poster.

—So is this how you endear women to you? Alice says. —Take them on a tour of the worst part of town?

—You're a rare breed, willing to take a walk with a stranger.

—Has it ever worked?

—I wouldn't know.

—So this is a first for you?

—There's a first for everything.

[2.4]

A dozen eIes peer out from the base of a building, each devouring the periphery, the view, each painted in neon colors, each calling attention to itself. If only the world knew, if only people stopped and stared and thought and considered the point of the eye above the 'i,' of the eIe as a whole, then their worthless trips down commuter lanes, their mechanical processions to and from work, might crack and dissolve. The illusion, the subjective world of lies, the lives of drone-like activity, of corporate controlled sanctuary, might fizzle and sizzle and fade away.

But then no one stops to gaze. No one stops to consider the eIes. Everyone drifts and ambles, everyone moves—to curbs and cabs, to buses and intersections. The eIes are there for all to see yet no eyes gaze at the eIes on the wall.

—They must have no lives, Alice says. —These things are everywhere.

She's clutching her arms at her chest. Her hair curls around her shoulders and bounce as she leans forward to study an eIe. Her eyes fold inward. Her lips curl. She seems innocent somehow, lost and delicate somehow.

—Would you be opposed to a proper date? I say.

—If this is your opening volley, I'm kind of afraid to see what you'd have in mind.

—Cliché: Dinner, maybe a movie. Something simple and traditional, something unoriginal.

—And if I say no?

—You'll never see me again. No hard feelings.

—But if I say yes?

—Then you'll see me tomorrow night.

She peels her eyes from the eIe and straightens her spine, allows her arms to drip and droop at her sides.

Universes are born and collapse, civilizations rise and fall, lives blink into and out of existence, in the seconds she burns considering my proposition.

[3]

Streaks of blood parallel chunks of bone and gristle, fifty metacarpals and proximal phalanges roast in rows atop a field of bile: the national symbol, adorning cars and chrysanthemums, people and landscapes, even lapels. Symbols of the efficacy of the inculcation of devotion, of supplication and submission. Through the perilous fight

16

of sight and disillusion, through the streams of movement and red anuses quivering overhead, through the mists of the deep frozen in moments of dread and regret, the blood and the bones and the bile merge and congeal, propagating delusions of simplicity, humility, and nobility.

And these symbols flutter overhead, hanging from poles piercing the chrysanthemums. Light from the sun sparkles inside these symbols; it projects their images onto the sidewalk, onto my feet, as corporate soldiers march beneath them. Every now and then, a soldier breaks his or her gaze and glances at the symbol, but their eyes are empty, ghostlike. What are they thinking? Does the symbol, the mere sight of it, reinforce the delusion, or does it trigger contemplation? If contemplation is triggered, it's probably a superficial variation—and in the end works to conceal inquiry and reinforce delusions of simplicity, humility, and nobility.

[3.1]

—They see what they want to see. We don't fit with their conception of reality so they choose, and probably not consciously, to overlook us.

—How do we break through?

—It's like evolution: gradual. But we'll affect them if we keep at it.

—Sometimes I believe that. But sometimes I don't.

—I'm here every day. Every day I'm out here doing this. And no one ever looks at me, and by that I mean no one pays attention to me. But they see me, whether they acknowledge me or not. And so I keep doing this. Every day. And then one day I won't be here. Maybe I'll be sick, maybe I'll be married or famous, or maybe I'll be dead. Then the people who walk by here every day, the people who see me without registering me, will notice something's different. They probably won't know something's different, but they'll feel it. The way you do when you leave the house and forget something, but you can't for the life of you remember what you forgot. And so it bugs you. One day, my absence will elicit that response. These people will continue to come by here, to pass through here, and whenever they do they'll feel this haunting, nagging sensation. And some of them will hopefully start to think. And some of those hopefully will begin to evaluate why they pass through here every single day of their miserable fucking robot lives.

[4]

Art is an activity.

The artist is a person engaged in the activity, in the moment of creation. We can only qualify the object itself as art—whether it's a story or a poem, a sculpture or a painting or a film, etc.—while it's in the process of being created.

Before it is created, an object of art is mere fantasy; the artist, a thinker; the activity, an abstraction. After it is created, an object is a commodity; the artist, a bullshitter; the activity, a memory.

To those who are passive in the arts—i.e., the viewers or the readers, etc.—the activity is the intention; the object, an ambiguity, something open to interpretation; the artist, a craftsman.

The act of creation—active—and the act of interpretation—passive—are distinct. A theory of art that doesn't take the distinction between the active and the passive into account is an incomplete theory.

[5]

Corporate soldiers march in phalanxes, crowding the sidewalk, the streets. The sound of their marching forces dread into the ever-thickening air. Obedient, some march with eyes forward, blank-faced, although many play with tablets or phones.

Through columns of cars, up curbs, through the columns marching down the sidewalk, two black haired beasts cut and dash and run. They weave between the pressed flesh of the marching drones. Soldiers refuse to acknowledge them, so the beasts cackle and leap into the air. Then they stop and stand and pretend to play with or speak on telephones, forcing the columns to slip out of formation.

The soldiers spit on the sidewalk or throw candy wrappers or cigarette butts on the ground, or they toss soda cans or bottles or plastic cups into garbage cans, and miss. They march forward without batting an eye.

The two beasts flank the phalanxes. One beast sticks a stencil on the side of the building, fills it with red spray paint. Someone shouts. Hey. A cop slips between the phalanx and shouts again. The beasts take off running. The cop follows them, kicking candy wrappers and cans and still-burning cigarettes as he chases them around a corner.

[5.1]

The stencil:
A red arrow pointing south, in opposition to the northbound drones.

[5.2]

I appear in a window overlooking the block. I touch my face and it ripples. A bee hiding in the crevices of flesh, now unspooled, now stretched, wiggles and writhes; it spins and floats away and disappears into the ocean shimmering in front of me.

Behind me, two suits wearing men tromp forward. Their voices float toward me:

—... computational automatism blooms black symbols on white voids ... ample desire to change perceptions ... see one thing differently, everything changes.

This block is spared from columns flowing to and from chrysanthemums, so I spin and sit on the sidewalk— leaning against a building—and light a cigarette. I'm sweating. The wind taps me, cools me. An ocean of doubt and anguish engulfs the ground.

The earth is a monument to persistent cataclysm. Scars are recognizable in pebbles embedded in the concrete. Billions of years of anguish trump petty material concerns, and so I jump to my feet and float while I smoke. The sky is blue, light blue, and the clouds are gray; they threaten to disperse debris—including pools of human cells. But for now they're benign. For now the columns march: I hear them a block away. South and north, east and west. For now I can finish my cigarette before dispersing beneath an awning.

The sky is still stubborn today.

[6]

And the eIe goes unnoticed. It watches everyone from every corner. Unlike the drones, the eIe isn't obedient.

Like them, it isn't subject to the whims of linear time, a secret they can't or won't acknowledge.

[7]

Then there she is: Alice, standing in the doorway. Then there she is: Alice, floating into the living room. Then there she is: Alice, peeling off her jacket. Her movements are lyrical. The quatrains of her motion soften the room, somehow brighten it. She experiments with mimicking the air, lingering between particles, hovering in elegiac machinations, and glances at the ceiling, challenging the vibrations with her eyeballs eyeing and her fingers fingering. The floor melts. The room accordions toward her, cowering beneath her as she bends light and evades the promise of perfection. With a smile, she persuades the particles to whip and spin stanzas in a blur; the motion of activity fuels the merger of Mimesis and poetry, and the forms protruding from the rhymes in her eyes capture the music, repeating the chimes in time to the writhing rhythm of the muted minute hand.

Then there she is: floating to the ceiling. Then there she is: taking my hand, carrying me to the roof. We land and sit and crawl onto our backs, lying side by side as we watch atmospheric warfare. Clouds form cannons, fire, explode. Mounds of corpses grow and dissolve.

Alice sees animals and children where I see chaos and destruction.

I kiss her without closing my eyes. Her skin is immaculate, the flesh of a God sculpted by Michelangelo. She kisses me. Her tongue is dry and tastes like pomegranates. I open my eyes and we're lying in bed, naked. She goes to the bathroom, returns with light spilling out of the bathroom. Shadows dismantle her face—then only outlines remain visible.

She slinks across the room and crawls into bed. The walls collapse. Now we're sitting in a villa eating Mexican food. Alice grins as she eats. I drink wine. My eyes return to her and we're back on the roof of my apartment building, sitting on the ledge, gazing at the emptiness below.

—It's hard to change the way I see things, she says. —I've been trying since that night, but I only saw things differently when you pointed them out.

—It takes practice.

—But how do I start?

—We learn to associate things. Have you ever looked at something, say a landscape, and said, 'That looks like a Monet' or 'That's like something out of such and such a movie'?

—Sure.

—We're trained to make those associations ... trained by people or non-conscious processes. A painting or a movie, or even a poem ... those are cultural institutions, which means those associations aren't hardwired. At our core, we're hardwired to seek patterns, and we see patterns everywhere, and we associate one kind of thing with a similar kind of thing ... associating a landscape with a painting of a landscape, say. Or, look out there, at the city. Now you may be inclined to see the lights and the buildings and think, 'It's like something out of a noir film.' A lot of people do just that. I used to. The key is to form an awareness: pay attention whenever you make those associations, and prevent them. Stop them or suppress them. Then open your mind and try to consciously make free associations. Like those lights over there: why would you compare them to lights in a picture or in a movie or to similar lights in a hotel you've stayed in; why would you compare them to lights at all? They're lights. Don't compare like to like; associate them with something random, with something un-light-like, to, say, a cantaloupe, or a cat skull.

—And that's what you did?

—Yes.

—But then aren't you just exchanging one image for the other? I was hoping for something more ... I don't know ... liberating, I guess.

—These associations aren't just for fun. They will make you see the world differently.

—But so what? she says. —I want everything to change.

—Everything will change. The world will become new again. Everything is constantly refreshing; everything is always new. You're a writer ... don't you want to present a fundamentally different world?

—I'd like to think that I do ... in my better moments.

—But with this you'll present something entirely different, I say. —And not just visually: there's a trick ... here's another pointer: deprive yourself of touch, of the sense of touch.

[8]

The steel of dust cracks the sky. Night bleeds onto the town, soaks buildings and streets in bile. Moon groans and swells and spits into its reflection. Clouds shimmer. Night ululates in the radiance of repetition. Worker drones evacuate the city. The nightly Armageddon flashes from block to block, guts the town, scatters debris. Nothing is fervent or alive. Business hours reduce chaos to memory. Sounds echo and ricochet from building to building, from street to street.

The unseen and the unknown, the unseeable and the unknowable, crawl from shadows into light dripping from streetlights. The whorl of day secretes new worlds at night, and the populace sprouts up and blossoms and clings to buildings and streets—coalescing amoebae split, spreading viruses, corrupting newborn universes writhing in the glow of the moon's bleached reflection.

[8.1]

I'm spotting Meat as he plasters a 12x12 portrait of Bill Burroughs on the front of a bank. The streets, silent, glow under the dome of streetlights. Cars crawl up and down the streets. No police are in sight, haven't been all night. But that doesn't stop Meat from peering over his shoulder every fifteen seconds or so.

　　　—Just finish it already, I say. —I'm here for a reason.

　　　—I can't go to jail again.

　　　—Then quit the distractions and eat your pork and beans.

　　　He's rolling glue over the portrait, ensuring the print will stay.

　　　—I feel that feeling again, he says. —Feel it?

　　　I do:

　　　Sounds nictate over the eye of the city. Cars and trucks roar—a block, two blocks away. The hollow thumps and thuds of silence, the pounding of hearts, fill the gaps. The streets are throbbing wounds bubbling with infections. Meat finishes applying his bandage to one such infection, says,

　　　—Things are breaking up again. They know we're here.

　　　—Finish the job.

　　　—I'm done.

Through the roars of the city, then through the silence, Meat slaps my hand and thanks me by jutting his chin skyward.

—I expect you'll return the favor, I say.

—I always do.

—We're close to a breakthrough.

—Says you.

[8.2]

I slip my hands into latex gloves and shake the can of paint. The spot tonight is on the side of a building across from City Hall. I press the stencil against the building and fill it in with black paint. Then I move over a few feet and repeat the process. Sixteen eIes are now staring at me and, more importantly, fixed to keep their eyes on City Hall.

Soon eIes will cover the town. Soon I'll be free—we'll all be free—to vanish into the folds.

[9]

Her touch recalls the fermented air of youth, how when I wanted to dream about my future I'd only go so far as to spray cum into the phantom writhing on my lap. Only now the phantom is real. She's a redhead, and she's on top of me, bathing in the silk of night as my milk darkens the pink of her flesh, somehow making it transparent.

She moans and pushes down on my chest. Her tits bounce. Her eyes are closed, her hair disheveled, bouncing, bouncing; she twists her neck, groans, and howls.

The specter of youth fades, fades. Everything becomes pale and blue and illuminated: her flesh on my skin, her breath in my face, her hair interweaving with mine. The past is an eyeball concealed behind a colorless lid. Nothing means anything except right now. The world vanishes. The light and sounds pouring into the window forestall the harbingers of newly hatched universes.

She rides me, she moans and rides me. The coil in my stomach and chest unspools.

[9.1]

She's lying beside me now. The sun screams into the room, announcing the dawn of the post-industrial age. Cars whine and buses howl. Feet slap concrete as voices rise, harmonize, and crescendo.

Stories unfold on the ceiling, but they're incomprehensible. They're incomprehensible because I'm too busy reading the prose encoded in the breath tickling my neck.

Her breath is soft, controlled, as if she's too self-conscious to breathe, as if she's afraid her breathing will trigger annoyance, or concern. She's lying near me, leaning into me. My arm is beneath her, curled around her. I interpret her breath and pull her to me.

And listen.

I listen.

Then words obscure images. Syntax and grammar, and refined imagery, unspool and dissolve in a sea of blackness: a hand fingers an open wound as the sky withers and droops inward. High overhead the sun blinks and the absence of light shimmers in the moment of the essence, when all things shrink and freeze and grope and gripe and convulse on the acid of tongues swimming in a sea of ichor. A man with a blank face skitters through a window—the glass ripples—and rushes toward me, but then he stops and spins and freezes: on his back are breasts, concealed in a halter top, and a blank face is in the back of his head. Hair curls down around the cheeks and chin and breaks against the shoulders. Shadows push into the face and a fist emerges—the wrist hangs where the nose belongs. The woman convulses and collapses. She lands on her stomach. The fist protruding from her face uncurls its fingers and crawls across the room, carrying the head and body. It stops in front of me. To tremble. Then the woman's legs, now at eye level, twitch and bend, and the hand pushes up, propels away from the floor, and the woman arches her back and lands on her feet, and— We're in a dome submerged in water. The woman and I are seated at a table, sitting on toilets, each shitting. Our shit floats through tubes and pollutes the water outside the dome. The woman watches her shit dissolve, and she smiles—she's grinding her teeth, moving her jaw horizontally. Then she opens her mouth—to speak?—and rocks tumble out and smack the tabletop. Each rock cracks open and spills snot onto the table. The snot bubbles and foams and transforms into a few dozen worms, each baring the head of a kitten. The kitten-worms mew, mew, and the sounds pulse and crack the glass on the dome. Water races through the cracks and fills the dome, fills the dome, and— and—

I listen. Listen.

Alice lies beside me. Her breath broadcasts the melody of a poem I can't deconstruct. And the tone of her message, shallow and oblique, slip into my pores and lulls me back to sleep.

[10]

Alice dips unleavened bread into hummus and pulls it to her lips. She flashes a glance at me as she slips the bread into her mouth. Then her eyes droop and melt and disappear behind two blue-painted eyelids. Mouth and eyelids each slow the clocks as they devour sustenance and amusement. Her eyes take a breath and fling open while her lips, still joined, bend upward, pleating the flesh on her chin.

She drags her pinky finger along the corner of her mouth. Taking another bite, she grinds and grinds and grinds, using her eyelids to mute her performance.

Red and white lights flash behind her, strobing people at their tables, each of whom chew and flutter and inject poetry, plucked from Sophocles, into the moment. A chorus of teeth scraping forks and clattering jaws, songs of reflections on strange evolutionary necessities. All faces blur the panoply of odors—of seafood and pasta, of meat and garnish—swirling in the room.

And then Alice takes another bite. She closes her eyes, smiles and chews. She grins in a sort of eye-opening tease, with a smile, with a squint. She tilts her head, allows her hair to tumble into her face. Flaccid and bemoaned. As she chews yet another piece, she whips her hair backward, pirouettes her hair, and milks the curtain call. A part reveals shoulders and a too-thin neck, sallow yet beaded with sweat. Inviting. But then another bite closes the curtain. The people at a nearby table chew and scrape silverware in a clattering chorus, and they mock and they tease me.

When she finishes chewing, Alice pushes the hummus aside and leans into the table. She glances at me without smiling. She smiles by narrowing her eyes, sucking her lips inward, piercing and freezing them. And visions erupt in her eyes: love, sex, conversations, each swirling in the reflection of fruit her gaze invites me to pluck. Yet her hands fumble and her neck shivers, her eyes waver and her chin trembles. It's a breathtaking performance, and I nearly applaud.

[10.1]

—So then why were they chasing you? she says.

—Because it's illegal.

—Can't they see it's art?

—They see statutes and ordinances. They see the respect of private property, and lack thereof.

—It shouldn't be illegal, she says. —I don't think it should be illegal.

—But if you legitimize it, then you can control the message. Banksy already ruined it. We're trying to take it back.

—What is the message? There's a message?

—Not a message; there are many messages. Unfortunately, a lot of noise drowns out what some people are trying to say.

—I can't see what anyone's trying to say.

—Okay, I say, —I chose my words poorly. They're trying to uncover certain possibilities, I suppose.

—What kind of possibilities?

—It's not for me to say.

—No?

—It's for you to figure out. The images are brands and the brands are only successful if you can associate them with something meaningful.

—So then it's not art, she says, —it's advertising.

—Marketing, advertising; it's propaganda.

—Selling what?

—The pleasures of an alternate reality.

—And you believe this? she says. —You believe in it?

I nod.

—And that's why you were helping out? You want to play your part in this, what, this opening of the doors of perception?

—Something like that.
—Have you ever been caught? Arrested?
—On more than one occasion, sure.

[10.2]

Night solidifies. Alcohol drags fog into the restaurant.

[10.3]

—Time is now, she says. —I'm tired and I want to go home, but at the same time I'm enjoying myself.
—We can go back to my place.
—I don't think ...
—It sounds forward and it sounds like a maneuver, but it's not. There's something I'd like to show you.
—I'll bet.
—My apartment leads to the roof. I'm the only one who can access it, the only tenant at any rate. Some nights I like to sit up there and examine the city. Inspect it. I'd love to show it to you.
—You're right, she says, —it does sound like you're maneuvering.
—I don't want this to end, at least not now. Come to my place, I'll show you I can be a perfect gentleman, and I'll even pay for a cab home.
—And you want nothing in return?
—I want only to show you what I see.

[10.4]

She pushes her chair back and stands. Her hair tumbles over her eyes, then she flings her head back, parts the curtains. The waitress, passing behind her, ducks to avoid a face-full of hair.

—Ready? Alice says.

I drop some money onto the table and stand. Then I take Alice's hand and we spin in a semi-circle. The room darkens, the walls and ceiling collapse. A field of stars commingle with fog overhead. We step forward. I close the door behind me. Alice releases my hand and walks away from me.

The city is a network of bioluminescent cells. They flash and fade and shimmer: pink and purple, red and orange and yellow. Life teeming with rage, with desire. Life fluttering behind closed windows or in cars, or bubbling on bicycles below.

I sit on the ledge and dangle my feet off the building. Alice slides behind me. She peers at the sidewalk below—her breast touches my shoulder, her breath scars the back of my ear.

—Sit. I smack the concrete beside me. —You won't fall.

—No, no. I can't.

—I won't let you fall.

—I don't think I can ... I've never been on a roof this high.

—Have you ever sat on a bench? in a park?

—Sure.

—Have you ever fallen off it?

—No.

—And you won't fall off this.

I tap the concrete.

She slithers to the ledge. I wrap my arm around her. She's shivering, trembling; her neck is stiff; she's burying her chin in her chest, holding her eyes closed.

—Don't look down, I say. —Look up. Open your eyes. Look at the snake over there.

—The what?

A snake writhes in the distance, on the other side of the arc-like underpaint bleeding into purple and blue fog coagulating the sky. Its scales are bioluminescent; colors and lights pulse and contract.

—See it? I say. —The snake.

—I don't ... She's scanning from left to right, up and down.

The horizon is nearly imperceptible. Fog obscures it. Streetlights, house lights, headlights shine and flicker and fade on the other side of town. I trace the horizon with my finger, curving it to emphasize the horizon's snake-like spine.

—I ... yeah, she says. —It does kind of look like a snake. And the lights are like scales, like slimy scales reflecting the sun maybe, like maybe it's hiding in a bush.

—Ready to strike.

—The moon.

—That's good. 'The horizon is a snake preying on the moon.'

—Sounds like a poem.

—We'll call it Alice's poem.

—It has to be more traditional, like 'An Ode to Alice.'

—'Alice's Lamentation.'

—'Alice's Lamentation,' she says. —I like that.

Scales transfer from the snake to Alice's eyes. They warp the gloss. Convex bubbles flip and pervert the scales. She smiles—the scales crawl; bioluminescent membranes cover her eyes.

The scales enchant and entrance me and pull me forward. I kiss Alice. She kisses me. Then the building slips away and we float in darkness, in absolute darkness; we float down, down, down, landing in my bed, naked, in the blistering glow of transmutation.

[11]

The eIe doesn't know time. Time doesn't know the eIe.

[12]

It's what we don't say:

Discover the temperament and the disposition of a culture by examining what they refuse to discuss. In a city such as this, where money is power, where supplication to the master is virtuous, it's easy to slip into the gaps between what is acknowledged and suppressed, and read the impressions seared into the psychology of the masses.

Look at the system:

It teaches children what to think and calls it education. It demands education as a means of participating in the 'global economy.' Education is not meant to enlighten, to teach children how think, to distinguish logic from fallacy. Children are taught what to think and told when to think it—parameters are established, and they're trained to act within these parameters, punished or shunned for daring to venture outside them.

Chart our growth:

As children, we're taught we can be anything, then we're persuaded to announce, in preschool or kindergarten, our lifelong ambitions. What do we want to be when we grow up? A fireman or an artist, a doctor or a police officer—the question is rigged; it inculcates a lesson society reinforces: not only is work inevitable, but it's noble. To succeed, we're taught, you must take personal responsibility. If you don't take responsibility for your actions, if you don't do what you're expected to do, then you are lazy or uneducated or somehow ignoble.

Language is a closed system:

It is not a component of the universe that obtains. Language is an intellectual virus we spread from person to person; it affects, and sometimes alters, our neurophysiology without infecting a universe independent of human beings. Our thoughts are not expressions of unique, ineffable things locked inside us, things we cannot communicate. Our thoughts are components of a tool—language. Yet we view language as if it contains some special meaning; we treat language as though it is somehow intangibly connected to that which obtains. These views are consequences of consciousness—we can use the metaphor 'delusion' to 'describe' these consequences.

Language is transferred from person to person, and it stays within them. It is a loop encircling another loop—people. It can be perceived through the senses, transferred through some senses, but it doesn't obtain independently.

Natural language is arbitrary:

Language is what we call sounds we're trained to project, individual and idiosyncratic sounds produced by manipulating the air flowing into, and out of, the throat and chest—we manipulate the air by manipulating the vocal folds or opening or closing the glottis. As cultures, we agree to use certain sounds in certain ways. We train—and are trained—through example: prolonged exposure to natural language trains us to use it, and once we've learned how to use it, we master it.

But while we retain the ability to use it, we don't retain the details of our training:

We are assaulted by language from birth onward. Each moment of every day presents the possibility—and probability—of exposure; we mimic the sounds and then we mimic how they're used, but we don't remember—we can't remember—the minutes and the minutia of every experience or encounter with natural language.

This form of source amnesia blinds us, and it encourages delusions, such as natural language has 'meaning.' You could say these delusions are internalized, and the 'meaningful properties' of natural language trigger something like a placebo effect.

So then we internalize certain concepts, which are tricks of language, and are duped into 'believing' they're components of reality:

If you're taught the earth revolves around the sun, you might take that sentence to represent 'reality'; but it doesn't represent reality: 'the earth revolves around the sun' is not a component of reality; in reality, these are things that simply obtain, yet through language we're fooled into believing that 'the earth revolves around the sun.' In reality, 'the earth' is a thing that obtains, 'the sun' is a thing that obtains, the relationship between 'the earth' and 'the sun' is something that simply obtains. The sentence 'the earth revolves around the sun' is not composed of magical words that somehow reach out and grab things that obtain.

Language doesn't connect us to things that obtain; it's a wedge that divorces us from them:

If you stand in a room filled with Chinese students who speak only Mandarin and say, 'The earth revolves around the sun,' you will not employ language to latch onto its subject and transfer this intangible component to those students. There are no intangible components linking natural language and things that obtain. If you uttered that sentence to a roomful of Chinese students, you would have accomplished nothing.

You speak English, they speak Mandarin; to them, you're producing noise.

But delusions persist:

Natural language is culturally inculcated and reinforced. It is not linked to things that obtain; it is a loop encircling another loop—people; yet you delude yourself—you treat language as though it has 'meaning,' and you assume these 'meanings' somehow 'reflect' 'reality.' The delusion triggers something like a placebo effect, so when you're trained to use the sentence, 'America is a bastion of freedom, liberty, and democracy,' you might delude yourself into thinking that this sentence reflects something like 'reality.' When you're trained to praise corporations and slavery to consumerism, when you're trained to articulate and trade these phrases, you might delude yourself into thinking that those sentences reflect something like 'reality.' When you're trained to praise the rich and the famous, when you're trained to condemn or dismiss the tired, the hungry, the poor, you might delude yourself into thinking that those sentences reflect something like 'reality.'

And if you become tired or hungry or poor, your situation might trigger negative psychological responses. And if the rich or the famous do not align with your delusions of them, or if corporations or consumerism do not align with your delusions of them, or if America doesn't align with your delusions of it, then negative psychological responses might be triggered, or you might reject those things that obtain in favor of the 'reality' of the 'language' you've been trained to use.

[13]

Everything is broken, decayed. The streets are filled with glass and flesh, growling harbingers of the future. A woman walks toward me. She doesn't see me. Her eyes are hollow, their colors fade. Her flesh is baked. Rings beneath her eyes undulate.

A crowd moves, flows around me. I slap a stencil against the wall, spray it black. Then I peel the stencil away and disappear into the crowd. A man glances at me as I cross the street. His eyes are pale rods and cones spinning in a riverbed.

I hit the sidewalk on the other side of the street and, sitting on the corner, light a cigarette. Something rustles behind me—a predator stalking the jungle. I spin: a woman hunches at the periphery of the columns of corporate soldiers; she's digging through a bag. She's one of them, a soldier, dressed in the fatigues of high finance.

I snake through the crowd and stop behind her. Overhead, a canopy flaps against the building. Meat wall with metacarpals and proximal phalanges swimming in bile, blood, and bone. It flaps, flaps, fucks the wind.

—Excuse me, I say.

The woman's eyes fold inward. She straightens her spine.

—What does that say to you? up there?

I point to the meat wall. Her eyes tap it—long enough to acknowledge it—and then they slam down, toward me.

—Opportunity, she says. —Freedom.

—How often do you see those?

—Is this like a survey? she says. —Are you a journalist or something?

—Yes. Absolutely.

—Now what was the question?

—How often would you say you see one?

—Throughout the day. They're everywhere.

—Since adolescence?

—Since birth. Easily.

—And to you it symbolizes freedom and opportunity.

—And liberty, she says. —The free market. Everything great about our species.

—Okay, so without looking, now keep looking at me, don't look at it, will you answer one more question?

She nods.

—How many white stripes are on it?

—Thirteen. No, wait ... white?

She glances up. I click my tongue.

—No cheating, I say.

She flutters her eyebrows.

—Now that I think about it, she says, —I never pay attention to it.

[13.1]

Alice and I: only the eIe keeps track of time.

[13.2]

—Now look: every single person down there is a musician. Every one. So within that group, no one distinguishes themselves by saying, "I'm a musician." Of course they're musicians, or they wouldn't be here. We can only define ourselves by distinguishing ourselves from other people. You and I are not musicians, they are; so they're defined by distinguishing themselves from us. But within that group, taking us out of the equation, within that group, they don't define themselves as musicians because they're all musicians.

—But not everyone plays the same instrument. The pianist probably distinguishes himself from the cellist.

—But he wouldn't say, "I'm a pianist" and she wouldn't say, "I'm a cellist" in this scenario. They're at their instruments. He's playing the piano. Now you can't present me a scenario in which he plays the piano and says, "I'm a pianist"; or while she's playing the cello, she says, "I'm a cellist."

—What if they're being interviewed for a radio show?

—While they're playing instruments? If they're being interviewed for a radio show when they're not playing instruments, then the game has changed. I'm talking about this game, here and now, with just those people down there. Now, while he's playing the piano or while she's playing the cello, can you think of a possible scenario in which he or she would need to say, "I'm a pianist" or "I'm a cellist?" Can you think of a scenario in which the negation would be true? Could you envision a scenario in which, while playing the piano, he says, "I'm not a pianist?"

—But he's playing the piano right now, she says.

—And she's playing the cello. Doesn't that distinguish them from each other?

—Action and language are components of the language-game. But in the sense of self they each carry in their heads, these distinctions are linguistic. Yes, his action of playing the piano distinguishes him from her, and her action of playing the cello distinguishes her from him. The mechanical act of playing a piano does not turn on the hinge of any internal or external dialogue. If you were to go down there right now and ask him how he's doing that, how he's playing that song, there's a good chance he'll respond by saying something like, "I don't know." He's been trained to play that piano, and through rehearsals he's been trained to play this song. These are mechanical actions, I say, —and while the process of mechanical actions, such as playing the piano, is underway, there's no need for him to conceptualize himself as a musician, at least not in this moment. Only when he stops playing, when he glances at the cellist or the violinist, or up here at us, can he begin to lay the groundwork for drawing distinctions. And these distinctions won't be broad; he won't say "I'm a musician"; he might narrow the language and say I'm a pianist, but there'd be no reason to do so; he just finished playing the piano. His actions alone don't necessarily allow him to use those actions as a basis for his sense of self. In that moment. Other people can call him a pianist, I just did, but that's a distinction I'm using to distinguish him from the cellist. He probably can't hear me right now, so my characterization of him, for the time being at least, probably has no effect on his sense of self.

—But he is a pianist, she says, —and I'll bet money he defines himself as one. What you're saying doesn't make sense; are you saying his sense of self excludes what he's doing right now? His sense of self probably doesn't change from one minute to the next.

—It does. Our sense of self is a story we construct to help us wade through possible scenarios our brains construct every second of every day; it's built on a foundation of subjective experience, and it's ad hoc.

—But it feels wrong, she says, —like your argument is one-dimensional: no one's sense of self is comprised of one thing.

—That's the point I've been trying to make, I say, laughing. —Our sense of self is a pastiche comprised of many components, and no one component is predominate at all times. We emphasize different components in different scenarios, which means that our sense of self is malleable and liable to change.

[14]

The walls message my head. The room entombs my gloom. Embodies it. From floor to ceiling: everything shudders. Day knocks on the window and drifts inside. Cold air flows from the vents, and hums, whirs, screams.

The color of music splatters against the walls. The stench of sunlight seeps through the glass and molds water, transforms it into ice.

A version of me stands erect in a mirror. Frozen in a rigor mortis shell. He sees what I see: an infinity of me. The millionfold uncountable innumerable us each stare into the other's eyes and contemplate crossing over, climbing through and slipping into the eyes of the other.

We've each done it before. A thousand times. Wandered into the mirrored eye and emerged through an eIe in the street—and thought we were home for good. Then the machine started again—always the machine restarts—and shattered our hopes, dismantling our illusions.

—Today is not the day, I say.

A thought follows: but when? when will time and space vanish and collapse and reform? when will people see us for what we are—and not what they perceive?

Hogwash.

A fantasy.

A misconceived perception of reality.

[14.1]

Steel trees planted in a sidewalk. They tower over the streets, spit in shame at night. But they're closed in daylight: they can't shame or tame anyone when the sun blasts her rays down here.

A steel tree, somewhere near the center of town, calls to me. A stencil of a decapitated cartoon cat is painted on its trunk; the body clutches a sign reading, 'aristocrat'; the cat's head—with X-shaped eyes—lies next to the body; it's wearing a top hat. Below it, someone wrote, with a marker: 'That's crap.'

It doesn't work at all, this image. It's too literal. Anyone looking at it can see a point is trying to be made, which will lead them to automatically infer a point—not necessarily the point. If they infer a point with which they disagree, they might reject the image; if they infer a point about which they're uncertain, then they might retain the image to reinforce or condemn a theory or an argument; and if they infer a point with which they agree, then they might not 'need' the image because they've already retained the 'point.'

In open cultures in which we teach by mapping language—aural stimulation—to behavior, people can be misled when others teach them, through repetition, to map specific language to specific behaviors. But in closed cultures—cultures within cultures, such as street art—our prop art works by mapping visual stimulation to behavior. Introducing language into the mix comes later. How it arrives is the key: if someone's told what a picture means, then they might reject it, or they might accept it without having processed the explanation; but if, over time, they map kinds of language to these images, then they might experience something like an epiphany.

This is our goal.

At least it's my goal.

Teach them to associate the eIe with certain behaviors, reinforce this association through repetition, and sooner or later—I hope—they'll parse the association until they find themselves questioning their behavior.

And they'll do this by individually mapping language to the association.

But some people haven't figured this out. Some people fill the city with shit because the movement is self-replicating, and, for most, the motivation is lost.

I pluck a Magnum marker from my pocket and fill in the sign, eliminating the word 'aristocrat.' Then I stand back and examine the decapitated cat holding a black sign.

It's shit, but at least it's no longer literal.

[14.2]

Meat is at the printer making copies of 20x20 murals he's going to plaster somewhere. The images are massive black and white magnifications of the Ebola virus, but a double image is superimposed into it, burying Christ on the crucifix in the cells.

A pink-haired woman leans against a counter, watching Meat cut away the excess paper. Her eyes are canyons: hollow, unkempt, breeding diamonds. She curls her wrist inward, toward her chin, as Meat shoves a wad of paper into a garbage can.

Of the two, she's the first to notice me.

I've been standing in the corner behind Meat for at least a minute. Pink smiles and breaks her slouching lean. Meat follows her gaze.

—The hell's going on, man? he says.

—Looking for help to hang something big?

—I've been trying to get Pink to help me.

—I print them, Pink says, —and leave the 'art' to you fools.

—When are you going out?

—Tonight, he says.

—I'll help you and you can get my back tomorrow.
—Sounds good.
We shake on it ... like it matters.

[14.3]

The sun blisters the asphalt. Sunlight bounces from window to window, setting the city on fire. Trees tremble. Grass tangoes. The faces of worker drones glow dead white, ashen, and the wind reconstructs the valley into an alto sax archipelago.

Children hang from windows. Some bounce from rocks. Their screams scatter fish in aquariums lining a mezzanine atop a rundown pharmacy. I encounter images everywhere I go: the city is a burlesque waiting to be discovered, the city is a painting waiting to be explored. The city is more than the economic structure it pretends to adore. But too many faces are rotted and gutted, too many eyes are sick and jaundiced and near sighted. Irises breathe and snap shut. Brains fold inward when confronted with alien or unfamiliar imagery. Snakes rise from avocado colored ashcans and squirm to the heavens, bisecting and dissecting and bifurcating clouds—two of which clench into powderpuff fists. And glints of steel, of yellow and cobalt reflections, sprout wings and pierce the clouds, and the clouds shape-shift: the fist becomes a lion; the lion's jaw opens, extends until it snaps; and both pieces of the face dissolve into an acid-blue sarcophagus.

Down below, on the scarred and pleated earth, lottery tickets grow from trees. Pylons of blood and excrement boil with the glory of homo habilis, homo erectus, homo sapiens, whose screams bend space and time, leaving signatures like fingertips dragged along a still-drying canvas.

[14.4]

A phone call from Alice:

—Hey, she says, —my boss is making me stay till close. Do you mind if we push our little get together back, say 9:30, 10 o'clock?

—Actually, yes; that gives me a little more leeway. A friend asked for help and I've been concerned about time.

—We could reschedule.

—I'm not busy; now I'm just passing time with him, waiting to see you.

[14.5]

The breath of steel and sheet metal mingles with the stench of trash and decayed wood. Night has descended now. Streetlights uncover shame, deflecting regret again. Two beast-like men amble down the street, disguised in soil and old clothing—parting gifts from a civilization indifferent to the needs of the many.

Wisdom cracks and the city melts in waves. The buildings are insect skulls, free of flesh yet preserved. The stench of death permeates the city, yet everyone's alive as they navigate the dungeons at night. Faces are foreign here. The enigma of anonymity mocks the call of the creation of currency, and no one is afraid to open up and scream. Here, the drones are of a different sort: oil-eyed monsters lubricated with the juice of experience and doom, wandering through the rotted corridors of a museum preserving the skulls of ambition.

Then there's the face, the human face.

Twenty feet tall and twenty feet wide, the Ebola virus, with hidden Christ on a crucifix, is a Rorschach test. In it I see the face of a beehive-man rolling his eyes into the back of his head. His mouth open, pinched downward, a scream frozen, and preserved and recorded for our ancestors to stumble on, and wonder, what frightened him.

Meat is rolling adhesive onto the front of his piece, which is now plastered to the side of a transnational financial institution. I've been standing a few feet away, hunched in the shadows, casing the streets, searching for cars or pedestrians. The oil-eyed monsters, on occasions when they pass, shoot their eyes sideways— but they look through us. Night quivers. The tools of the police state are dismembering the corpse of Lady Liberty on the other side of town, apparently.

—Shit, goddamn it, Meat says.

He's holding his roller like a scepter, studying his work.

—It's fucking crooked, he says. —Goddamn it.

—It'll have to do.

—Fuck that.

—What are you going to do, peel it off?

—Or die trying.

He picks the corner until it curls; he tugs it, but the paper doesn't rip. Roars stall him; before I can spin to investigate the humming noise, I watch Meat drop his roller and flee. I follow him, pumping acid and adrenaline through my chest and into my skull. Behind me, sounds like shivering tin rips across the street. The sounds of dull thuds, of feet slapping sidewalks, spiral outward. Corporate gangsters chase me. They squeal into two way radios. Their guns and gadgets rattle inside their belts, corkscrewing into my ears.

Nothing blurs but the world goes dark, a trick my brain plays to preempt the hassle of motion blur. And in the gaps of vision, images are recreated: buildings beside me, headlights and taillights of cars swimming in the concrete, sidewalks and streetlights and people leaping out of my way. Everything is fluid. Everything is static. But detonations rock my body. Nerves fray me; they fry and sizzle.

Meat is gone and I'm still running. Behind me, someone shouts something. Don't move or stop or something. I leap over a cinder block wall and jump onto a parked car. A cop is behind me, shouting and slapping the ground with his feet. He says something again, an order. I leap from the car to the second floor of a parking garage.

I shatter a wall of shadows dissecting the levels and rocket up the ramp to the third floor. Shouts behind me, but no footsteps. A siren screams a few blocks away.

The jaw of a building protrudes from the ground beside the garage. An overbite-ledge hangs above the window fangs. Shadows and light dance and splay atop the fangs. They produce a visual symphony, a soaring screeching aurora borealis of a hallucination. Fingers open and curl. Eyebrows fold. Smiles erupt and tongues unfurl. The faces call to me, seem to beg me to greet them.

The shrill shouts of the cop below push me forward, and I'm three or four steps into a sprint before I realize what I'm doing. Then I jump. From the parking garage to the ledge of the building beside it, I jump—and I hit the ledge and grab a pipe to balance myself.

The cop's voice marries the sirens as I launch into the alley and blast through shadows, vanishing into the blistering night.

[15]

Screams roar through the labyrinth. Chrysanthemums groan. Corporate soldiers march, march, through the tin can crosshatched ziggurat of forced gratification. Sunlight splinters and cracks the dome overhead, which springs leaks.

Sunlight pours in.

[16]

A woman hangs from a window over the street. Two, maybe three, stories above the sidewalk. She's hanging from a cord—elbows stiff, fists clenched. A skintight unitard reveals her breasts and cunt, each rib, every curve and dimple. She swings back and forth, back and forth. A featureless white theater mask obscures her face. Eyeholes allow sunlight to bounce off her eyes, which sparkle.

She swings back and forth, back and forth.

She sings as she swings—a trilling howl, an atonal screech, beautiful in its compulsion.

People march to work. Men and women carry briefcases and bags, play on phones or tablets, hustle north or south, east or west; many cross or sidle along the sidewalk. No one glances at her. No one seems to know she's there.

Gears in a machine are not capable of hearing their squeaks or mistimed thumps.

[16.1]

The woman stops swinging, hangs from the cord. She lowers her head and gazes at me—her eyes shine through the eyeholes, radiating heat.

I wave.
She gazes.
I lay on the sidewalk and wave.
People flow around me.

The woman splays her legs and spins. She flips her arms and catches the cord and climbs into a nearby window.

[16.2]

A blind drops and blocks the sun.

[16.3]

Lying on the sidewalk, I stare at the clouds, at the gray and black wall filtering the light of the sun. Faces crawl by me. People flow around me. Flesh screeching in the machinery of the moment, all automatism and no verve. Screams and screeches and howls—silent yet audible. Meat machines programmed for busy bee antics.

Below me, the ground roils and rumbles, flops and floats, as though I'm lying on a waterbed. I perch my arms behind my head and close my eyes. Light taps my eyelids. Pink bleeds into black. Smells of diesel fumes assault me. The hum of stomping feet, of marching corporate soldiers, relaxes me.

Then I feel it, a shadow growing over me.

The white-masked woman is standing beside me, hunched over, staring at me. Her hair—knitted into a ponytail—hovers between us. Her eyes break through the darkened holes in her mask. She studies me, her eyes comb over me, her breath smacks her mask, vibrates it.

It implants chills on my spine and arms.

—You can see me? she says.

—Watching you, up there, was like listening to poetry.

—But how can you see me?

—The same way you see me, I suppose.

I get to my feet. White Mask jumps back, hunches. Her forearms tighten.

—What do you call it? I say. I point to the cord.

—Loneliness. Confusion.

—I'd call it beauty.

She and I raise an island from the trembling earth. The sea of busy bees doesn't penetrate our cliffs.

—Would you like to see beauty? she says. —And loneliness? And confusion?

—Absolutely.

—Then come with me.

[16.4]

She leads me into her building, up a flight of stairs, and into her apartment. Roses grow in the walls. Clocks are planted in the floor. Couches and chairs hang on the ceiling or sprout from the walls. Sculptures of flowers and legs—without genitalia—are drying in the corner of the room.

I'm standing on a clock, watching time squirm beneath me, when White Mask crosses the room. She stops near the window, back to me, and pulls her arms from her sleeves, wiggling out of her unitard.

Her back is smooth, like glass, and it ripples— fills the glass with rainbows and bubbles—when she contracts her muscles. Mask still on, she stands in front of the window, backlit by the haze of the sun. She's darker, faded—a double exposed form languishing inside a silhouette.

She says something. The mask muffles it.

—I don't know, I say.

In that mask, only her eyes are alive.

—Would you like to see it now? she says.

—This isn't it? I brush the air between her body and me.

—You can't see it from here.

She opens the window, crawls onto the sill. Then she climbs onto a perch outside and disappears.

I slip out after her, follow her from windowsill to windowsill, up and over four stories, to the roof. A billboard as wide as the building sprouts from the rooftop. White Mask climbs another story; she sits on the platform at the base of the billboard—still naked—and swings her legs to and fro.

I sit beside her, catch a glimpse of the city: glass, concrete, and steel; man made chrysanthemums towering over the land; concrete grows on horizons, blurs the curves and melts the edges.

Below, streams of worker drones scurry. Cars and buses god the streets. Feet-slapping thunder and murmurs, engines and horns float up, up, enshrining us in the symphony of routine.

The face of a woman beams on the billboard behind us. Airbrushed, practically painted, the woman is smiling beside a logo and a slogan promising more bang for my buck. She stares off into space, frozen in a drum beat of recycled air.

A horn rises. Tires screech. A car below nearly slams into a bus. A half dozen cars riff in similar keys, and the bus makes a hard left, turns into an adjoining street. People clotting the sidewalks flow and flow. The line churns forward, ever forward. No one stops or pauses or turns their heads.

—Millions and millions of people, White Mask says, —and yet no one notices me. They never acknowledge me. How do I know I'm not dead?

—Are you afraid?

—Sometimes.

—Then you're not dead.

Eyeballs swell behind the mask.

—How do you know you're not dead? Do they ever see you?

—I don't think so.

—So you might be dead, too. Maybe this is our eternity. Condemned to silence and anonymity.

—If so, I would say this is heaven, not hell.

—Look at them down there, she says. —Just look at them: always on the move. I swing and swing, or I sit up here, like this, naked, and still they don't notice me. If we're not dead, maybe we've been sucked into a parallel universe.

—They see what they want to see. We live outside their realm; they can't squeeze us into any picture they might have.

—Or they're simply incapable of seeing us.

—It's not that they're incapable; they've spent so much time ignoring us that they can't see us any longer. But this is temporary.

—How do we get them to see us?

—We make them confront our traces, I say. — We leave signatures in space and time, signatures from which they infer us.

—But then, to them, we're not alive. To them, if they infer us, we're merely hypothetical.

—It's a start.

—I'd prefer to be dead than to be a nameless and faceless, a featureless, figment of someone's imagination.

—I'd rather be a figment of the imagination than dead, I say. —And how do you know we're not a figment of the imagination? here and now?

—If we were, then someone would acknowledge me.

—I'm acknowledging you.

—But what if I'm dead and you're part of my eternity?

—Do I feel real to you? Right now?

She brushes my cheek, lowers her hand to my hand. She slips her fingers into my fingers, weaving a flower, which blooms when she unfurls her fingers.

[17]

A man sits on an apple in a park, gnawing on a plank from a bench. He's wearing hats on his knees and a knee pad on his head. A group of bicyclists pass him—the bicycles: screaming chunks of metal—as they race to collide with the intersection. The man coughs or clears his throat whenever a bicycle passes him.

He drops the plank and clamps a match between his lips. Then he presses a cigar to the match, shakes the cigar, and tosses it to the ground. He glances around as he mimes pulling smoke from the match.

Not a single pair of eyes flutter toward him.

I sit on the bench and light a cigarette. Smoke snakes into the atmosphere.

The man spins toward me, still seated on the apple, and, smiling, says,

—You again.

—Me, I say.

—You're disrupting my work.

—I'm validating it.

—Only they can. He points to a column of corporate soldiers marching up the street. Their faces point forward; their eyes glimmer with the empty light of routine.

—But they never look, I say. —I don't know if they can see us anymore. I don't even know what the fuck they do see anymore.

—They see what they want to see. We don't fit with their conception of reality, so they choose, and probably not consciously, to overlook us.

—So how do we break through to them?

—It's like evolution, he says: —gradual. But we will affect them if we keep at it.

—Sometimes I believe that. But sometimes I don't.

—That seems to imply that today is the latter.

—Maybe.

—Not 'maybe'; if you're not experiencing it, you wouldn't have said it.

—Everything has changed and yet no one realizes it, I say. —We need to break through to them. Urgently. But they won't listen. They can't if they don't even acknowledge us. How the fuck do we break through to them?

—I'm here every day, he says. —Every day I'm out here doing this. And no one ever looks at me, and by that I mean no one pays attention to me. But they see me, whether they acknowledge me or not. And so I keep doing this. Every day. And then one day I won't be here. Maybe I'll be sick, maybe I'll be married or rich, or maybe I'll be dead. Then the people who walk by here every day, the people who see me without registering me, will notice something's different. They probably won't know something's different, but they'll feel it. The way you do when you leave the house and forget something, but you can't for the life of you remember what you forgot. And so it bugs you. One day, my absence will elicit that same response. These people will continue to come by, to pass through here: and whenever they do, they'll feel this haunting, nagging sensation. And some of them will hopefully start to think. And some of those hopefully will begin to evaluate why they pass through here every single day of their miserable fucking robot lives.

 —But we need brevity not longevity. It's crucial.

 —'Truly, it is impatience, the mother of folly, who praises brevity.'

 —Brevity is the soul of wit.

 —Wrote Shakespeare ... in a five hour play.

[18]

In a corner in my bedroom: a canvas on an easel. I'm adding the finishing touches to a flag carved into the side of an elephant. The elephant is a mutant, its rear end replaced by a donkey. The elephant-donkey machine towers over glass and metal chrysanthemums wilting in a concrete ocean. Cells—covered in three-piece suits—swarm the bases of the chrysanthemums.

 The bones of palms and the lowest sections of fingers have replaced the stars on the flag; I'm putting the finishing touches on the proximal phalanges—the lowest sections of fingers—with a daub of gray paint textured to simulate bone.

 Sounds rush into the window: cars and horns, music and conversations. I feel them, the auditory rush slipping into the window, flicking my flesh, and I try to ignore them, but their touch is too much, the tactility of the sounds fluttering into the window force me to drop my brush and shut the window.

Noise, all noise. Conversations with the void, with the moment, with the event horizon of the void as it refuses to record every nuance and detail.

I pick up the brush, texture the paint, but the moment—my moment—has slipped into the void; it's vanished.

Great.

Distraction has retarded the time meant to finish this painting, crammed it into the crevices of that slab of meat behind my eyes.

[19]

—But so what? she says. —I want everything to change.

—Everything will change. The world will become new again. Everything in it is constantly refreshing; everything is always new. You're a writer ... don't you want to present a fundamentally different world?

—I'd like to think that I do ... in my better moments.

—But with this you'll present something entirely different, I say. —And not just visually: there's a trick ... here's another pointer: deprive yourself of touch, of the sense of touch.

—Like that's ... is that even possible?

—Not fully, no.

She picks at a rock embedded in the ledge.

—See? I say. —Like right there. What compelled you to touch that?

—Habit, I guess.

—Yet you're not certain.

—I'm not. No.

—Whether you know it or not, touching something like this ledge gives you a greater sense of understanding the object, so when you see something similar to this from afar, your judgement or understanding of it is altered because you can add depth to it. You know similar objects are solid yet coarse. This helps your cognitive faculties build a more three-dimensional model of it. Tactility, I say, —the sense of touch, does affect how we perceive things. Michelangelo thought sculpture was superior to painting because pigment on a canvas produced an optical illusion; three-dimensions within a painting were a gimmick; realistically, the paintings were still abstract. But a sculpture presented three-dimensions, and you could verify that by touching it, even if you're exploring something subtle like the definition of a muscle in a forearm.

—I don't see how depriving myself of touching something will alter how I perceive it.

—It won't alter how you perceive it, but it could, I think, allow you to associate more freely. Deprivation can, I think, help you make *a priori* associations instead of *a posteriori* associations, which expands the realm of possibilities.

—But it doesn't change reality. Whether or not I understand fully what concrete is, that concrete is still objectively concrete. Independent of me.

—No, I say. —Everything obtains. Everything simply is. But when it comes to you, nothing is independent of you. To you, everything is subjective; everything is filtered by you, interpreted by you; this entire conversation, and everything you 'see' right now, everything you 'hear' and 'smell' and 'touch,' are models constructed and reconstructed by your brain. And I'm telling you that you can train your brain to present these constructions differently. It's like a sort of cognitive cubism. Here, let me show you:

[19.1]

The canopies beneath the sea quiver as the flowers moan overhead. Faces linger and dwell in the fluorescence of the shade. Alice and I stroll up the sidewalk, past a group of ghosts huddling in an alcove; they're whispering, contemplating their reflections. Their whispers grow wings and flap overhead; they dissolve in the radiance of the twilight announcing the blooming sun.

A brick wall flows from a flower: it's bleeding, encrusted with gristle; palm prints mar the top right corner, residue of meat from the millions sacrificed to consecrate it. Another wall flows from another building. Yet another still swims in the window of a parked car.

—Tell me what you see, I say.

—Buildings. The sun's coming up.

—Over there. And there.

She scans the vicinity, squints, shakes her head.

—Right there, I say. —There. Anywhere.

—Flags?

—They're omnipresent, so common you see them without registering them, without consciously registering them.

—They're just flags.

—But what do they mean? Tell me what they mean to you.

—Freedom.

—See? These are associations you're trained to make. You're not working outside the system; the system's working through you. And it's such a common image, you no longer consciously notice it; and the association's so common you no longer consciously recognize it. Now look at it. When was the last time you really studied it?

She shakes her head.

—Now tell me what you see.

—Stars, stripes. Colors.

—Remove all content. Remove everything you've ever been told about it, and then tell me what you see.

She fixes her eyes on a meat wall above her.

—Interpret it for me, I say.

—I can't.

—Why not?

—It's ... I don't know ... an abstraction. Without associations, it doesn't mean anything.

—So then rewrite it. Affix new associations, free associations, and tell me what you see.

She spins in a circle, bounces her eyes from one wall to the next.

—I see a wing torn from an angel, she says. —I see blood dripping down the wing. The colors are like sign language, like the screams of innocence.

—Now above you, around you. What do you see?

She spins again, scans the buildings, the cars, the streetlights.

—Rusty nails protruding from a bed of wood, she says. —Or flowers, shiny flowers, waving. Asthma and anger. Despair rowing through the streets.

—What do you usually conjure when you glance at these buildings?

—I quit looking at them years ago.

—But what do you think, what do they usually mean to you?

—The triumph of capitalism? or progress? They're testaments to the ingenuity of humankind.

—Now dissociate those concepts.

—Everything is clustered, she says, —confused.

—But their size, their scope and presence tell you what?

—Success. Confidence. This is the result of conquering adversity.

—Dissociate from those concepts and tell me what you see.

—I see emptiness, arrogance, death.

—Now free associate new concepts. Describe what these associations make you want to see.

—The sky is cracked and broken. Steel and glass stalactites are dripping to the earth, burrowing into the ground. Their roots spread across the city, concrete and asphalt. Bacteria and viruses grow and evolve and scurry across it. I see advertisements and warnings signs, statutes posted. I see signs directing the flow of traffic. I don't see chaos, she says, —I see order. I see control.

She spins in a circle again. Then she sits on a curb and glances across the street.

—It's enforced uniformity. Everything. It's like a song or a symphony, an epic poem telling us that we're free, convincing us that we're free, and controlling ... defining ... every action, every desire.

She glances at her hands, says, —Every story I've written reinforces controls I was too blind to see. Every story I've written consecrates the illusion.

—So force hallucination, I say, —and write me a new story, a better story, a different kind of story.

Afterword

To write, to direct, to edit—my ambitions as a child, a teenager, a young adult. I wrote screenplays on a word processor, a sort of electric typewriter, and by hand, on a legal pad. In my early twenties, I acquired a Panasonic mini DV camera. I filmed everything, and soon this camera and I rarely parted. My friends and I shot skits, or I filmed random, everyday events. Once or twice, my friends and I made a short film.

The experimental and avant garde had intrigued me for most of my life, so, at one point, I designed a short film as follows: in lieu of writing a screenplay, I would write individual scenes on individual index cards, the scenes tied together thematically, then my friends and I would shoot those scenes. On completing principal photography, I'd shuffle the index cards a few times and then edit the film in that order, allowing chance to dictate chronology.

But about halfway through principal photography, my buddy, who "starred" in the short film, decided he no longer wanted to dedicate his time to the project. So I was stuck with half the material I needed.

As I said, I always carried my camera, and I had filled tapes with random shots—the sky, trees, children playing in a yard, my friends laughing, my buddy walking through the woods, and so on. So I catalogued some of this footage, wrote individual shots on individual index cards, replaced those cards with scenes we hadn't shot, and shuffled them. I even copied a couple scenes and shuffled them into the mix, as well, allowing chance to play with repetition, too.

After I shuffled the cards, I edited the film. I set the entire piece to music to obscure the jarring effect of sounds crashing from scene to scene—a choice I wouldn't have made had I edited that film later in life.

The final result intrigued me. It didn't work as I'd hoped because it was incomplete, at least as I had intended it. But on a level it did work: it was a somewhat hypnotic character study, a visual scrapbook, and an examination of the language of cinema.

Although I haven't watched that film in years, I've not forgotten it.

Some years back—maybe three, maybe five; I can't recall—I set out to adapt those techniques to the written word. I would write scenes, tied together thematically; I would number those scenes; then, when I wrote enough to fill a novel, about 60,000 - 80,000-words, I would write the number of each scene on an individual index card, shuffle the cards, and then piece the book together according to the random chronology.

But like the budding star of my film, I, the writer, decided to abandon the experiment. I abandoned it for two reasons, which I'll enumerate briefly: 1), much of the book centered on the surrealists' notion of eschewing estheticism, so I wrote much of it in a dissociative state; however, I had to write random gibberish for thirty to forty-five minutes each night until I reached a dissociative state, then I'd work on material for maybe five or ten minutes before I slipped out of that state; as a result, producing the necessary material proved exhausting, too exhausting for me to continue; and, 2), in writing a novel such as this, I didn't want a story or plot to drive the piece; I wanted themes to drive it; but I realized stories and plots were intruding as I continued to write.

So I gave up.

But unlike the short film, this project didn't stick in my mind. In fact, I moved on to other projects and forgot about it. Until recently. Going through old files, I rediscovered the pieces I'd written—about one-third of the low end of what I'd hoped to write. Reading it, I tried to imagine how it might feel when edited together. So I decided to piece it together. For shits and giggles, as they say.

As with the short film, I worked with what I had. I snuck in a couple short pieces from another—failed—project, and I repeated some bits; again, to see how chance would play with repetition.

Like the short film, I don't think the novella you just read worked—and you better have read it, you motherfucker; just kidding, I love you. But I don't think it was a failure, either. Some experiments are worth trying, even if you can't determine the results.

By chance, this novella ends in a way that I now interpret as a challenge, as a sort of throwing down of the gauntlet, and I leave that challenge here for you: So force hallucination, and write me a new story, a better story, a different kind of story.

Thanks for your time,
Daulton Dickey.

www.ingramcontent.com/pod-product-compliance
Lightning Source LLC
Chambersburg PA
CBHW070649130626
46555CB00006B/2776